This book belongs to

....

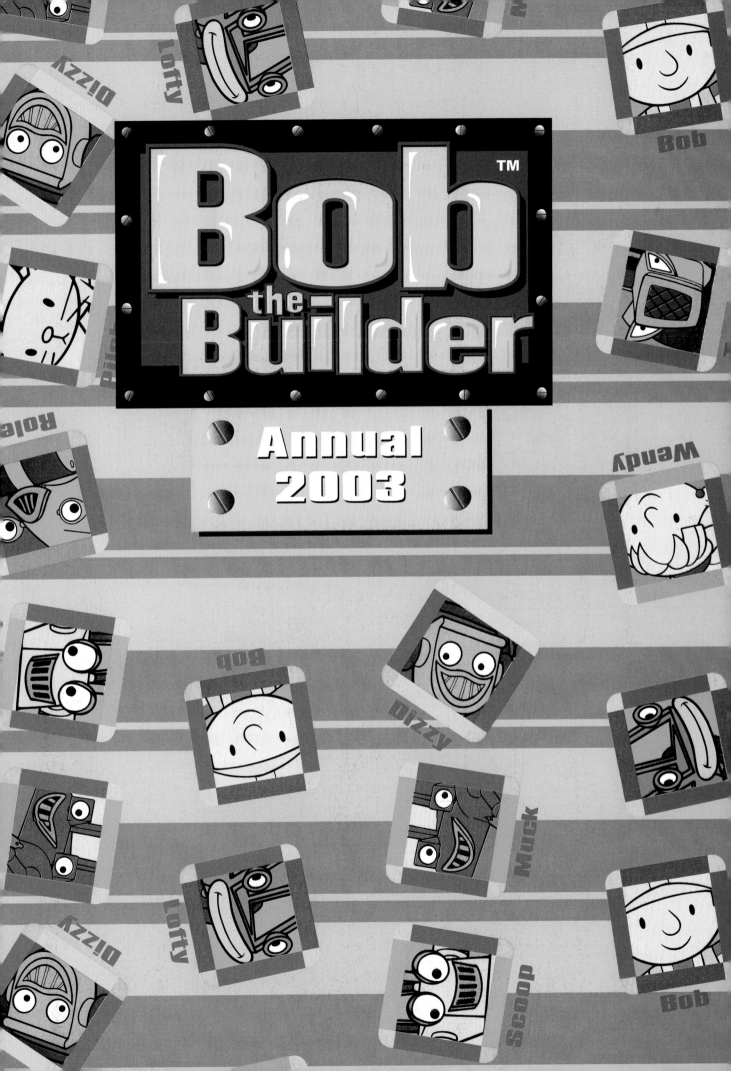

Contents

Written and edited by Brenda Apsley
Stories adapted from original scripts by Ian Carney,
Jimmy Hibbert, Simon Jowell and Diane Redmond
Designed by Sally Metcalfe

Based upon the television series **Bob the Builder** © HIT Entertainment PLC
and Keith Chapman 2002
With thanks to HOT Animation
Text and illustrations © HIT Entertainment PLC, 2002
The Bob the Builder name and character and the Wendy, Spud, Lofty,
Roley, Muck, Pilchard, Dizzy and Scoop characters are trademarks
of HIT Entertainment PLC. Registered in the UK. All rights reserved.

www.bobthebuilder.com

Published in Great Britain in 2002 by Egmont Books Limited,
239 Kensington High Street, London W8 6SA
Printed in Italy
ISBN 0 7498 5607 6

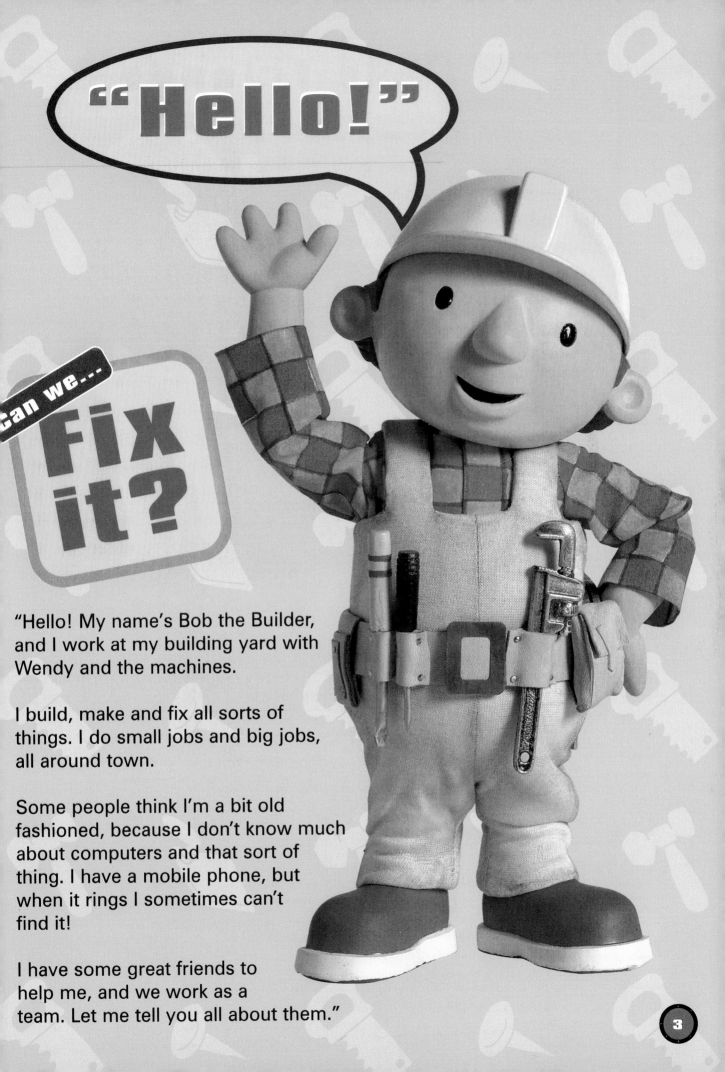

"Hello!"

can we... Fix it?

"Hello! My name's Bob the Builder, and I work at my building yard with Wendy and the machines.

I build, make and fix all sorts of things. I do small jobs and big jobs, all around town.

Some people think I'm a bit old fashioned, because I don't know much about computers and that sort of thing. I have a mobile phone, but when it rings I sometimes can't find it!

I have some great friends to help me, and we work as a team. Let me tell you all about them."

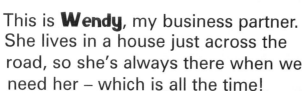

This is **Wendy**, my business partner. She lives in a house just across the road, so she's always there when we need her – which is all the time!

Wendy makes sure that we get to the right job at the right time, with all the tools and equipment we need. She's kind, patient – and she's a very good builder, too!

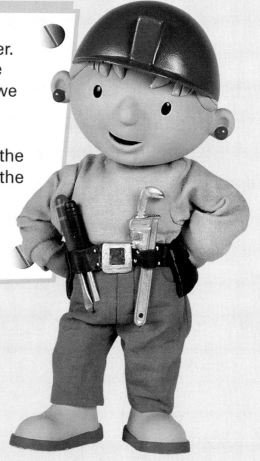

This is my cat, **Pilchard**. She's always hungry! And when she miaows we all seem to know just what she's saying!

Pilchard likes taking naps, but when she's awake she likes chasing things, especially mice!

You can usually find **Bird** sitting on the roof of the office in the yard or on top of Roley's cab, where he can keep an eye on things. He can't speak, but he lets us know what's going on using whistles and chirps.

Mr Bentley is the local building inspector. He checks the jobs we do. He likes things to be done on time – and he likes them to be done perfectly!

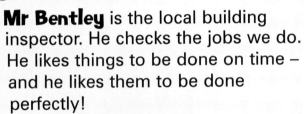

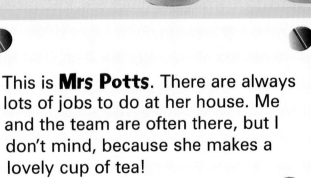

This is **Mrs Potts**. There are always lots of jobs to do at her house. Me and the team are often there, but I don't mind, because she makes a lovely cup of tea!

Scoop is a big yellow digger who's the leader of the team. He's like a big brother to the others, and he's always ready to help them, and to solve problems. Nothing is too much trouble for Scoop. But he's always ready to have fun and play tricks, too.

When I hear him say, "No prob, Bob!" I know things will turn out right.

Muck is a digger-dumper who likes to get as messy and dirty and muddy as he can. He loves being mucky, and that's how he got his name. He's scared of the dark, but his friends are always near to help him.

Muck sometimes does things without thinking, which can get him into trouble. But when I hear him say, "Muck to the rescue!" I know he's here to help.

Lofty is a mobile crane. He's quiet and a bit nervous, but he'll try most things with a bit of help and encouragement. Lofty is scared of just about everything, but especially heights, mice, and Spud the scarecrow!

As well as having a hook attachment, he has a grabber, and a big ball on a chain that we use to knock things down with. Very useful!

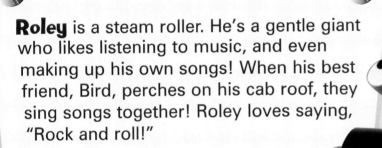

Roley is a steam roller. He's a gentle giant who likes listening to music, and even making up his own songs! When his best friend, Bird, perches on his cab roof, they sing songs together! Roley loves saying, "Rock and roll!"

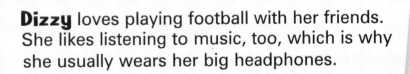

Dizzy loves playing football with her friends. She likes listening to music, too, which is why she usually wears her big headphones.

Dizzy loves dancing, and is always zooming around saying, "Brilliant!"

Dizzy is chatty, giggly – and she's always asking questions.

Farmer Pickles is a very good friend of mine. We do a lot of jobs at his farm just outside the town. He works hard, like us, and sometimes he helps us with our jobs, too.

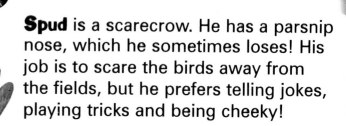

Spud is a scarecrow. He has a parsnip nose, which he sometimes loses! His job is to scare the birds away from the fields, but he prefers telling jokes, playing tricks and being cheeky!

When I hear him say, "Spud's on the job, Bob!" I never know quite what to expect. But if things go wrong – and they often do – we know he was only trying to help!

Farmer Pickles has a dog called **Scruffty**. He's cheeky and happy, and he's always getting into mischief. He likes chasing rabbits – and anything else that moves!

Scruffty likes my cat, Pilchard. They spend many afternoons at the yard or at the farm, playing and causing havoc!

Scruffty's Big Dig

One day, Bob was loading a bag of cement into Dizzy's mixer. "What are we doing today, Bob?" asked Dizzy.

"We're going to repair Mrs Broadbent's big bulge," said Bob.

That made Dizzy and Muck giggle. "Where is her big bulge?" asked Muck.

Bob smiled. "It's in the end wall of her house," he said. "We need to take out the damp bricks to stop the whole wall falling down."

Just then, Farmer Pickles arrived with Scruffty.

"Morning!" he called.

"Ruff, ruff!" said Scruffty. He wanted to go and play, so Bob took off his lead, and away he went.

Scruffty dug a hole in Bob's flower bed to show off to Muck.

"He's like me!" said Muck. "He loves digging!"

Wendy looked at her watch. "We'd better get a move on, hadn't we, Bob? There's lots to do today," she said.

"**RUFF!**" said Scruffty.

"Sorry, Scruffty, you can't come with us," said Bob.

"Dogs aren't allowed on a building site," said Muck. "Only machines."

Scruffty whimpered. He was disappointed.

"Never mind, Scruffty," said Farmer Pickles. "I'll give you a nice bone when we get home."

When Bob and the team got to Mrs Broadbent's house, Wendy looked at the wall. "We'll have to take out a lot of the old bricks," she said.

"But won't the wall fall down?" asked Dizzy.

"No," said Wendy. "We'll hold it up with some strong pieces of metal called props."

Bob and Wendy got to work. Wendy took off the old paint and plaster, then Bob put the metal props in place so that she could take the old bricks out. Then they started to lay the new bricks.

"Could you pop back to the yard for some more bags of cement, Muck?" asked Wendy.

"No problem," said Muck.

Scruffty was eating his bone when he saw two little rabbits. There's only one thing Scruffty likes better than bones, and that's chasing rabbits, so off he ran after them! But they ran down a rabbit hole.

"**RUFF!**" said Scruffty, and he started digging. His head and front legs were right inside the hole when the soil gave way.

"**OOOwwww!**" screamed Scruffty – and he fell into the deep, dark rabbit hole!

Muck was on his way back to the yard when he heard Scruffty's howls. "Ooh-er ... what's that?" he said.

He followed the howls to the hole. "Er, hello?" said Muck, peering inside.

"**Y-O-O-W-L!**" howled Scruffty. "**OOOWWWWW! OW-OW-OW-OO-OO!**"

Muck jumped. "It's a ghost!" he said. "**AAAHHH!**" He turned away, hurried out of the field, and rushed back to tell Bob.

Muck showed the hole to Bob and Lofty.

"**OOOOOO!**" howled Scruffty. "**RUFF! RUFF!**"

Bob knew the sound of Scruffty's bark. "That's not a ghost!" he said.

Muck knew the sound, too. "No, it's Scruffty!" he said.

"And he's got himself stuck down a rabbit hole," said Bob.

"**OOOOO!**" said Scruffty.

"Don't worry, Scruffty," said Bob. "We'll soon get you out."

But Bob couldn't reach him. The hole was too deep.

"Can you use your hook to lift Scruffty out, Lofty?" asked Bob.

"Er, yeah ... I think so!" said Lofty, and he lowered his hook, lower, lower, lower – until Scruffty was able to put his front legs around his hook.

Scruffty was soon safely out of the hole.

"We can't leave the hole like that," Bob said. "It's dangerous."

"But we can't fill it in," said Muck. "Where will all the little rabbits go?"

But the rabbits were busy digging a new hole. "They've already found somewhere else to live," said Bob.

"Right," said Muck. "Can we fill it?"

"**RUFF! RUFF! RUFF!**" said Scruffty. Yes we can!

When they got back to the yard, Muck and Lofty told Roley what had happened.

"Lofty was brave. He pulled Scruffty out," said Muck.

"But it was you who found him," said Lofty, kindly.

Just then Scruffty and Farmer Pickles arrived.

Scruffty dropped a big bone in front of Muck. "Scruffty's brought a thank you present for his best friend!" said Farmer Pickles.

"Thank you," said Muck. "It's lovely. But I don't really need a bone. Why don't you have it, Scruffty?"

"**RUFF!**" said Scruffty, and he started to look around for somewhere to put it.

"Don't dig another hole!" said Lofty.

Scruffty dropped the bone into the bucket Wendy was holding. "I'll put it in a safe place, and you can have it next time you're here," she told him.

"**RUFF! RUFF!**" said Scruffty. What a good idea!

"**RUFF! RUFF!**"

Count with Scruffty

Scruffty loves chasing things – even though he doesn't often catch any of them!

Can you help him count the numbers of owls, mice, tortoises and crows on these pages?

Clumsy Roley

In the yard, Lofty was lifting some planks of wood. "What's all this wood for, Wendy?" asked Scoop.

"It's for the decking in Mr Beasley's garden," said Wendy. "I need Lofty, Dizzy and Roley to help me."

"While you're busy with that, I'm going to fit a new kitchen for Mr Fothergill," said Bob.

"Can we fix it?" said Scoop.

"Yes we can!" said the rest of the team.

Mr Fothergill's new kitchen was in boxes. "It's in bits and – sniff! –

pieces," he said. "Sorry, some things make me sneeze."

Just then his pet parrot landed on his head!

"This is – sniff! – Hamish, my parrot," said Mr Fothergill.

"Parrot!" said Hamish.

Bob laughed. "I've never met a talking parrot before," he said.

"He never stops – sniff! – talking," said Mr Fothergill.

"Well, I'd better take this old kitchen out," said Bob. He opened his toolbox. "Spanner ... screwdriver."

"Screwdriver!" squawked Hamish.

When Wendy and the others got to Mr Beasley's house, he was waiting for them in the garden. He told Wendy he wanted the decking under the tree.

Lofty was looking at the tree when two squirrels ran down the trunk and on to his crane. "Oooer ... mice, with big bushy tails!" said Lofty.

"Oh, Lofty, they're squirrels!" said Wendy.

"Yes, they've got a nest in the tree," said Mr Beasley.

When the squirrels jumped on top of Roley's cab he decided that they were good fun. "Do you want to hear my new song?" he asked them. "*I like to rock, I like to roll...*"

As Roley danced, he rolled backwards and forwards – then rolled right over Mr Beasley's watering can! "You've rolled it as flat as a pancake!" laughed Mr Beasley.

"Sorry, Mr Beasley!" said Roley. "Clumsy me!"

Bob was busy putting the new kitchen units together.

Hamish, who was bored, decided to have some fun.

"BOB!" squawked Hamish in Mr Fothergill's voice.

Bob opened the kitchen door. "Did you call me?" he shouted.

Mr Fothergill came in. "No, I was working on my computer in the other room," he said.

"Oh, right," said Bob. "I'll get back to work then."

"SQUAWK! SQUAWK! SQUAWK!" said Hamish. It sounded as if he was laughing!

Bob was screwing the units together when he heard his mobile phone ring.

"BRRRRING!"

It was Hamish again, but Bob didn't know that!

Bob picked up his mobile phone. "Hello, Bob the Builder." But there was no one there!

"BOB!" squawked Hamish in Mr Fothergill's voice.

Bob put down the phone. "Coming, Mr Fothergill," he said.

"BRRRRRING!" said Hamish. **"Hello, Bob the Builder."**

"Just a minute," said Bob. "There's something funny going on here." He looked at Hamish. "You're playing tricks on me, aren't you? I'm never going to get finished if you keep disturbing me, so ... I'll put on my ear protectors."

Roley was busy in Mr

Beasley's garden. He rolled the ground flat, but he got a bit carried away – and reversed into the tree! "Oh no!" cried Roley. "I've knocked the squirrels' nest out of the tree. I'm so clumsy!"

"Don't worry, we can fix it," said Wendy, and with some spare wood and her tools, she made a new house for the squirrels. "Can you lift it into the hole I've dug, Lofty?" she asked.

"Er, yeah ... I think so," said Lofty.

"Now you can fill the hole with cement, Dizzy," said Wendy, "and Roley can roll it flat!"

Roley rolled the cement very carefully.

"Good job!" said Wendy. "You see, you're not always clumsy!"

The squirrels ran in and out of their new house. "I think they like it!" said Lofty.

"Yes, they do," said Wendy. "Right, we've got this decking to finish."

When Mr Fothergill went into his kitchen, Bob was still wearing his ear protectors. "ALL FINISHED!" said Bob in a very loud voice.

"No need to – sniff! – shout!" said Mr Fothergill, lifting one of the earpieces away from Bob's ear. He sneezed. "Oh, dear – sniff! – I hope the – **at-choo!** – wood isn't making me sneeze."

Mr Beasley really liked the decking, and he liked his new squirrel house, too.

"It's a pleasure, Mr Beasley," said Wendy. "Come on, team. Time to pick up Bob."

Roley wanted to say goodbye to the squirrels, but he wasn't looking where he was going. He rolled right over Mr Beasley's flowers!

But Mr Beasley wasn't at all upset. He showed Roley a scrapbook. "Look, my hobby is pressing flowers. I put them in the book – then squash them flat. Could you help me by rolling over the whole book?"

When Wendy and the team got to Mr Fothergill's house, Bob had all the old units stacked up ready to take to the recycling centre. "But the boxes might be too big to carry," said Bob.

"No problem, Bob," said Wendy. "Roley can roll them flat."

"Well, Roley – can you squash them?" said Bob.

"You see, Roley," said Wendy, "you're not always clumsy!"

Bob and Roley took Mr Fothergill's old kitchen units and the boxes to the recycling centre. Bob and Wendy always take as many things as they can, so that they can be used again.

Look at the little pictures at the bottom of the next page. Talk about what they are. Which of them can Bob and Wendy put into the bins to be recycled? Point, and say the names of the items.

road sign

tins

cake

newspapers

ladder

bottle

ball

pumpkin

bucket

"It was great to see you all at my live stage show. We had great fun turning a rubbish tip into a bandstand and putting on a show!"

Spud the Dragon

1 Spud likes dressing up. "Ha-haar!" he says. "I'm Long John Spud, the pirate!"

2 Spud dresses up as a cowboy. "Yee-ha! The Lone Scarecrow rides again!"

3 Spud finds a dragon costume. "Now I'm Spud the Dragon!" he says. "Roarrrr!"

What does Spud the Dragon do next?

Look at the pictures and talk about what you can see. Tell the story in your own words. Don't forget to make lots of funny dragon noises!

4

5

6

1 Bob had some great news for Wendy and the team. "My twin brother, Tom, is coming for Christmas, all the way from the Arctic!" he told them.

2 Bob had lots to do. First, he had to cut down a big Christmas tree and put it up in the town square.

3 Out in the forest, Bob's mobile phone rang. It was Mr Bentley. "A meeting with the new mayor? Right now?" said Bob. "OK, I'm on my way!"

4 Thousands of miles away, in the snowy Arctic, Tom was busy and excited, too. He was packing for his trip and Pogo, his husky dog, watched eagerly.

5 Roley and Dizzy were at the airport. They had gone to see their favourite group, Lennie and the Lazers, who had just arrived home after a world tour.

6 "We're going to the studio to work on John's new song. We're going to sing it at our Christmas concert in the town square," Lennie told them.

7 "I write songs," said Roley. "You do? Then why don't you two come with us?" said John, the band keyboard player. **"Rock and rolllll!"** said Roley.

8 But Lennie had a cold, and John was having trouble writing his new song. "How do you write your songs, Roley?" he asked. "I sing about what I see..." said Roley.

9 "...like these squirrels – squirrel rock!" John smiled. "I don't think that's quite what we're after," he said. "Have you got something a bit catchier?"

10 When Bob got to the town hall, Mr Bentley took him to meet the new mayor. She had lots of jobs for him to do, and they all had to be done at once!

11 "Banger, Lennie's roadie, is here to help you put up the Christmas tree, the lights and to build a stage for the Lazers concert, Bob," said the mayor.

12 "And you'll dress up as Santa to give out the presents, won't you, Bob?" said Mr Bentley. Bob gulped. "Well, can you fix it?" said the mayor.

13 "Tree ... lights ... concert ... stage ... and a Santa outfit," said Bob. Phew! It was a lot of work! "Er, yes, I think so ... " he said.

14 Tom was on his way to the harbour on Scoot, his yellow snowmobile, when he found a tiny reindeer all alone. "Oh dear, we'd better find your dad," he said.

15 Tom and Pogo found the reindeer on a ledge down a deep cut in the snow. Tom climbed down with a rope, and Scoot pulled him out.

16 By the time they rescued the reindeer, Tom had missed the last boat! **"Oh no!** I'd better go and radio Bob with the bad news," he said sadly.

17 Bob was very upset when he heard Tom's news. It wasn't going to be such a great Christmas after all. "Oh well, I'd better get this work done," he sighed.

18 When Lennie saw how upset Bob was about Tom, he had a great idea. He and Wendy flew off in his jet plane to the Arctic to pick up Tom!

19 As the small jet plane swooped over the town square, it started to snow. A few minutes later Lennie arrived in his limo.

20 But Lennie wasn't well. He had lost his voice! He couldn't sing! Roley had an idea, and he whispered it to the rest of the band.

21 "Why don't you sing your new song, John?" suggested the rest of the band. John was very nervous but as soon as he started to sing the audience went wild!

22 "And now," said the mayor, "will everybody please welcome ... Santa!" Bob was in a panic. "Oh, no," he said to Roley. "I forgot I had to be Santa too!"

23 But Santa was already there! And his sleigh was filled with lots and lots of presents!

24 Santa said, "Is Bob the Builder here?" When Bob went forward, Santa took off his beard. It was Bob's brother Tom! **"TOM!"** said Bob. "But when ... how ... ?"

25 "It's a long story," said Tom. "But I haven't even done the shopping yet!" said Bob, opening his present. "Don't worry, it's all taken care of," said Wendy.

26 "Well, thanks everyone," said Bob. "This really is going to be **THE BEST CHRISTMAS EVER**!"

"Christmas is a very special time of year. I've got gifts for all my team. Pilchard and Scruffty are helping me sort them out.

How many gifts are there on this page? Count them! Don't forget the one I'm holding and the one Pilchard is standing on!"

We've got lots of fantastic prizes to give away, courtesy of
acing Champions and HIT Entertainment Plc.

he 1st prize winner will win ...

is fabulous Bob Helmet Playset.
ip the lid to reveal Bob's world
 miniature, and play with Bob
nd Wendy down on the farm,
 the yard or on the construction
te.

50 runners-up will win ...

copies of Bob's White Christmas Videos,
featuring 5 super stories:
- Bob's White Christmas
- Lofty to the Rescue
- Wallpaper Wendy
- Wendy's Big Match
- Dizzy's Statues

How to enter:
All you have to do is to count the number of gifts on page 38.

Write your answer, and your name, address and age, on a postcard or the back of a sealed
envelope, then post it to this address:

Bob the Builder Annual Competition
Egmont Books Limited, Unit 7, Millbank House, Riverside Park, Bollin Walk, Wilmslow, Cheshire SK9 1BJ
Entries must reach us by 24 January 2003.

ules
- The winners will be chosen at random and notified by post.
- The judges' decision will be final. No correspondence will be entered into.
- The winners' names will be made available from Egmont Books (on request) after 3 February 2003.
- Please enclose a stamped addressed envelope.
- Employees (and their relatives) of Egmont Books and associated companies are not eligible to enter.
- Entries are limited to one per person.
- The competition is open to non-residents of the UK, Channel Islands and Ireland.
- The publishers reserve the right to vary prizes, subject to availability.
- The closing date for entries is 24 January 2003.

Cock-a-doodle Spud!

Bob and Muck are making a hen house for  .

Farmer Pickles

"The  will like it," says Bob.

hens

Farmer Pickles and  have a  .

Scruffty   basket

There are **4** eggs in it.

four

"My hen laid the ," says Farmer

eggs

Pickles. "Will you look after them while I find her?"

"Yes," says Bob, and he puts the in Muck's digger.

eggs

"Ooooo ... er!" says .

Muck

There isn't enough felt for the hen house roof. "We'll go back to the yard for some," says ![Bob].

Bob

"But what about the eggs?" asks .

Muck

"We'll find someone to look after them," says ![Bob] .

Bob

When Spud and ![Travis] arrive, Bob asks them to take care of the eggs.

Travis

"How can we keep them warm?" says ![Travis] .

Travis

Spud points to a duvet on the washing line. "We'll use that."

But ![Spud] stands on the duvet, and tears it! He's covered in feathers!

Spud

Just then, **1** of the eggs cracks open,
one
and out pops a  ! "Cheeeep!"
chick

"The chick thinks you're its mum, Spud!"
says  .
Travis

Spud puts the  and the  in his
jumper.
chick   eggs

When Bob and  get back, Spud
is fast asleep.
Muck

 wakes up when the big cockerel
Spud
says, "COCK-A-DOODLE-DOO!"

Bob puts the  into the hen house.
eggs
Farmer Pickles finds the mother  .
hen

"And here's Dad, the cockerel," he says.

"COCK-A-DOODLE-DOO!" says the .

cockerel

"Is that noisy thing their dad?" says Spud.

 barks at the , and it flies

Scruffty

cockerel

up into Spud's arms!

"COCK-A-DOODLE-DOO!" says the .

cockerel

"Oi!" says . "Get off! I'm not a

Spud

 !"

hen

"No, but you're a cock-a-doodle-scarecrow!" says . "Ha, ha!"

Farmer Pickles

"Ruff, ruff!" says .

Scruffty

"Spud's on the job! This is trickier than it looks! Can you help me find the little pieces of jigsaw that fit into the big pictures? Point to them."

Bob and the Big Freeze

One winter morning, the machines woke up to find that it had been snowing. The town and the fields were under a deep, soft carpet of snow.

Dizzy was very excited, and she whizzed around the yard.

"YIPPEE!" she said. "I love snow! We can build snowmen and have snowball fights, and ..."

"But there's work to do before we have fun," said Bob. "The wind blew some of Farmer Pickles's trees down last night so he wants me to cut them up for firewood."

"Can I come with you and Lofty?" asked Dizzy. "Pleeeeease?"

"OK," said Bob. "You can carry my chainsaw."

"I've got a job to do, too," said Wendy. "Mr Bentley needs us to clear the snow from the country lanes."

"I can use my snow plough!" said Scoop.

"Right," said Bob. "Let's go."

"Can we fix it?" asked Scoop. **"Yes we can!"**

"Er, yeah ... I think so," said Lofty.

Farmer Pickles showed Bob the trees that had blown down. "I'll cut them into logs," said Bob, getting his chainsaw ready. "But chopping up trees can be dangerous, so can you look after Scruffty, please, Dizzy?"

Scruffty wanted to play so he raced off and Dizzy had to chase after him.

They met Spud near the duck pond. It was covered in a layer of ice. "Look at me," said Spud, skidding across the ice. "I'm Spud the Skater!"

Spud spun around as fast as he could, but he lost his balance and landed with a thud!

Dizzy and Scruffty couldn't help laughing.

Poor Spud! He tried to get to his feet, but his legs kept sliding away from him, and – **THUD!** – he landed on the ice again. But this time there was a loud cracking sound, and the ice started to split.

"This is dangerous!" said Dizzy. "Stay with Spud, Scruffty. I've got to get help!"

"Oooer," said Spud. He didn't dare move, even though his bottom was feeling very cold. "Hurry, Dizzy!"

By the time Bob and the others got to the pond, Spud was on his feet again. "I'm all right now!" he said, but he lost his balance and landed on the ice again – **THUD!** There was a very loud crack, and the ice started to break up even more!

"Can you reach him, Lofty?" asked Bob.

"Er, yeah ... I think so," said Lofty. He tried to grab Spud by his belt, but missed him. He tried again, and this time he got Spud back on to dry land.

Just then a family of ducks waddled up to the pond.

Scruffty barked at them. **"RUFF! RUFF! RUFF!"**

"That's right, Scruffty," said Travis. "Ponds are for ducks, not scarecrows!"

"QUACK! QUACK!" said the ducks.

"But they can't swim on a frozen pond, can they?" said Dizzy.

"And the POOR ducks can't find anything to eat," said Bob.

"Neither can the other birds," said Dizzy. "Look, that one's pecking at the snow. Can we do something to help them, Bob?"

"You know, Dizzy, I think we can!" said Bob.

Meanwhile, Scoop was trying to clear a big snowdrift when his snow plough hit something metal buried in the snow. "I'd better dig it out," said Wendy. "I wonder what it is? It seems to be some kind of tunnel."

Scoop saw a fallen road sign and lifted it with his rear scoop. "Look," said Scoop. "It's a picture of a hedgehog."

"It's the hedgehog crossing Bob built," said Wendy. "And look, here are the hedgehogs that were sleeping in there. They're shivering with cold."

"Shall we put the hedgehogs back inside?" asked Scoop.

"No, they'll only go back to sleep when they're ready," said Wendy.

"But it's too cold to leave them here," said Scoop.

"Then we'll have to take them back to the yard," said Wendy.

When Wendy got to the yard, Bob was filling Dizzy's cement drum with bird seed. He told her about the ducks having nothing to eat.

"We got a bit distracted, too," said Wendy. "These hedgehogs were fast asleep and we woke them up by accident. They need somewhere warm to stay."

"And I know just the thing," said Bob.

"Great!" said Wendy. "We'll finish off the jobs and see you later!"

When they got back they told Bob what they had done.

"I cleared the roads," said Scoop.

"And Farmer Pickles has enough logs to last the winter," said Wendy.

"I fed the ducks!" said Dizzy.

"I've been busy, too," said Bob. "I've made a bird table for Bird and his friends, and a hedgehog house. I'll fill it with straw, then give the hedgehogs some of Pilchard's cat food to eat. There you are – your new home!"

The mother hedgehog hurried inside, and so did her babies.

"They like it, Bob!" said Roley.

"Yes, I think they do!" chuckled Bob.

1 Farmer Pickles and Scruffty are going to be in a dog show.

2 Scruffty does some tricks. "Lie down, Scruffty!" says Farmer Pickles.

3 Scoop wants to enter Pilchard in the dog show. But Pilchard is a cat!

What happens next? Look at the pictures and talk about them. Tell the rest of the story in your own words.

4

5

6

This is **JJ**. JJ owns the building supplies yard. I buy all the building materials I need from him. He's very friendly, and he really likes all the things he sells. He can talk about things like spanners for hours and hours! JJ likes to keep his yard neat and tidy, with everything in its place.

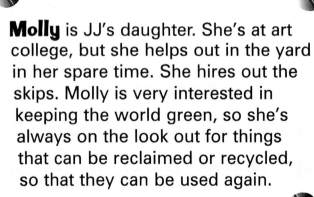

Molly is JJ's daughter. She's at art college, but she helps out in the yard in her spare time. She hires out the skips. Molly is very interested in keeping the world green, so she's always on the look out for things that can be reclaimed or recycled, so that they can be used again.

Skip delivers skips to JJ's customers, then collects them when they're full and takes them to the dump. He enjoys his work, and loves JJ and Molly. He's always happy when they tell him they are pleased with his work.

Skip can also carry things like pallets using his chains.

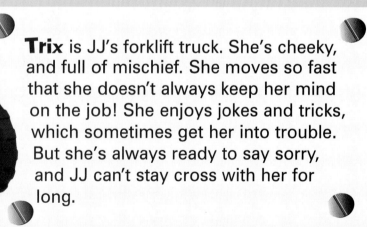

Trix is JJ's forklift truck. She's cheeky, and full of mischief. She moves so fast that she doesn't always keep her mind on the job! She enjoys jokes and tricks, which sometimes get her into trouble. But she's always ready to say sorry, and JJ can't stay cross with her for long.

The Egg and Spoon Race

Muck, Dizzy and Roley watched as Bob ran along the street outside the yard. He was holding a spoon with an egg in it.

"Why is he doing that?" asked Muck.

"I don't know," said Dizzy. "But look – Wendy's doing it, too!"

Mrs Percival, the school headteacher, knew what was going on. "Bob and Wendy are practising for the egg and spoon race," she told them. "It's part of the town Fun Day."

Bob and Wendy tried hard to keep their eggs on the spoons and run at the same time, but they bumped into each other, and the eggs fell to the ground! Luckily they didn't break, because they were hard boiled.

"I'm glad you're practising," said Mrs Percival. "Mr Sabatini's going to make a special giant pizza for the winner."

"OOOh, you've got to win!" said Dizzy.

"We'll try!" said Wendy. "Before the race starts, let's get some work done. We've got to put in some new doors at Mr Sabatini's pizza shop. Bob, if you and Muck pick up the new doors from JJ's, Dizzy and Lofty can come with me and we'll start taking out the old doors."

"OK, Wendy," said Bob.

"Can we fix it?" asked Scoop as they left the yard.

"Yes we can!" replied the others.

At JJ's yard, someone else was practising for the egg and spoon race – JJ! He ran along with an egg on a spoon as Molly, Skip and Trix watched.

When he went inside, Trix looked at his egg. "I'm going to be in the race, too, you know," she said. "Look, my prong's just as good as a spoon!"

She scooped up JJ's egg and spun round and round. "Trix can win it!" she said.

Trix was still whizzing around when Bob and Muck arrived. Trix whizzed in front of Muck, and the egg rolled off her prong, but clever Muck caught it in his scoop!

"Nice catch, Muck!" said Bob. "Good job it's a hard boiled egg!"

On the road next to Farmer Pickles's farm yet another person was practising for the egg and spoon race. Spud was supposed to be delivering a carton of eggs to JJ, but he wanted to win the race, too. But the egg he was using wasn't cooked, so when it rolled off his spoon, it broke, **SPLAT!**

"Oops!" said Spud.

When Spud got to JJ's yard with the eggs, Trix was very pleased to see him. "Eggs!" she cried. "Put one on my prong, Spud!"

Spud wasn't sure. "They're for JJ to cook with, not for you to run around with," he told her.

But Trix wasn't going to take no for an answer. "Oh, go on, Spud," she said. "Pleeeeese?"

Spud gave in, and put an egg on her prong.

She whizzed around, but the egg flew off, and landed, **SPLAT!**

"Again, Spud!" said Trix.

She whizzed around again, and the egg broke, **SPLAT!**

Spud laughed. "This is fun!" he said, putting another egg on Trix's prong.

SPLAT went the egg ...
and the next one ...
and the next one ...!

Soon all the eggs were broken! That's when Trix and Spud noticed what a mess they had made of the yard.

"JJ's not going to be very happy," said Skip.

"No," said Spud, looking around. "Erm, I'm going now. I've got lots more eggs to deliver!" And he ran out of the yard.

When JJ came out and saw the yard, he could hardly believe his eyes. "What on earth ...?" he said.

"Sorry, JJ," said Trix. "I was practising for the egg and spoon race with the eggs Spud brought for you, but when I dropped them, they broke, not like yours."

"That's because these are fresh eggs," said JJ. "You need to use a hard boiled egg, like mine. And you've got to learn to control it. Look, I'll show you ..."

When Spud got into town, he saw Bob and the team putting in the new doors at Mr Sabatini's pizza shop.

Wendy was telling Muck how the glass stayed in the wooden frames. "We put this sticky stuff, called putty, on the frame, then press the glass onto it. It hardens up and holds the glass in place."

Spud overheard what she was saying. "Heh, heh," he said. "Sticky stuff, eh? Just what I need! Spud's on the job!"

When no-one was looking, Spud took some putty and put it on his spoon. Then he pressed an egg on top. "Now I'm sure to win that yummy giant pizza!" he said.

When it was time for the egg and spoon race, all the runners stood in a line.

When everyone was ready, Mrs Percival said, "On your marks, get set – **GO!**"

Bob and Wendy got off to a good start – but so did Mr Beasley. He ran past Mr Bentley, and accidentally knocked his egg off his spoon!

"Oooohh!" said Mrs Potts as she wobbled, and her egg rolled along the road.

Soon there were eggs everywhere!

Trix raced as fast as she could, but it was Spud who was first across the finishing line.

"Giant pizza here I come!" he said, waving his spoon around in the air – with the egg still stuck to it!

"But your egg's stuck to your spoon!" said Bob.

"Spud! What's under your egg?" asked Mrs Percival.

Spud grinned. "Er, I used a bit of ... er ... sticky stuff to stop my egg falling off ..."

"Spud has been cheating," Mrs Percival told the others. "So now the winner is – Trix!"

"Fantastic!" said Wendy.

"Well done, Trix," said Bob.

"Bella!" said Mr Sabatini. "And eer she is – the firsta prize – mya giant pizza!"

The pizza was enormous! Trix lifted it on to her prongs to show everyone. "Thanks," she said. "There's a slice for everyone ... even Spud!"

Wendy's Photo Album

"There are lots and lots of pictures of Pilchard in my photo album! Look carefully. Can you help us find the odd one out? Point to the picture that is different."

"There's a page of photos of Bob in the album, too. Can you find two that are just the same, and point to them?"

"I need someone to help me put up all of these Christmas lights," says Bob.

Who does Bob choose to help him? Follow the tangle of wires with your finger to find out, and say the name.

"Goodbye!"